THE NEXT PANDEMIC:

What's to Come?

John Allen

ReferencePoint
Press®

San Diego, CA

© 2022 ReferencePoint Press, Inc.
Printed in the United States

For more information, contact:
ReferencePoint Press, Inc.
PO Box 27779
San Diego, CA 92198
www.ReferencePointPress.com

LIBRARY OF CONGRESS CATALOGING-IN-PUBLICATION DATA

Names: Allen, John, 1957- author.
Title: The next pandemic : what's to come? / by John Allen.
Description: San Diego, CA : ReferencePoint Press, 2021. | Includes
    bibliographical references and index.
Identifiers: LCCN 2021021598 (print) | LCCN 2021021599 (ebook) | ISBN
    9781678201722 (library binding) | ISBN 9781678201739 (ebook)
Subjects: LCSH: Epidemics--Juvenile literature. | Epidemics--Environmental
    aspects--Juvenile literature. | Communicable diseases--Environmental
    aspects--Juvenile literature. | Climatic changes--Health
    aspects--Juvenile literature.
Classification: LCC RA648.5 .A45 2021 (print) | LCC RA648.5 (ebook) | DDC
    614.4--dc23
LC record available at https://lccn.loc.gov/2021021598
LC ebook record available at https://lccn.loc.gov/2021021599

CONTENTS

An Eye on Future Pandemics

As he delivers daily lectures on COVID-19 and its deadly impact, David Aronoff keeps one eye on the future. Like his colleagues in immunology, he knows that another pandemic is not just likely but almost inevitable. Aronoff, director of the Division of Infectious Diseases at Vanderbilt University Medical Center, studies potential threats from pathogens around the world. Experts estimate that nature holds about 1.67 million viruses, of which perhaps 4,000 have been identified. Already, contacts between virus-carrying animals and humans are increasing due to loss of habitat, population growth, climate change, and other factors. Global travel means that an outbreak can race around the world within weeks. A sudden outbreak like COVID-19 can overwhelm the richest nations and leave their health systems struggling to catch up. And poorer countries can face health crises that quickly spiral out of control.

Coronaviruses are not rare, typically causing mild to moderate upper-respiratory illnesses like the common cold. However, SARS-CoV-2, the virus behind COVID-19, is called a novel coronavirus because it was previously unknown and people had no immune defenses against it. Experts worry that similar viral threats in the future could pose an even greater danger than COVID-19. "What keeps me up at night is that another coronavirus like MERS [Middle East respiratory syndrome], which has a much, much higher mortality rate, becomes as transmissible as covid," says Christian Walzer, executive director of health at the Wildlife Conservation Society. "The logistics and the psychological trauma of that would be unbearable."[1] As Walzer notes, the death rate for COVID-19 infection is low—less than 1 percent—while the death rate for MERS is about 35 percent. Mortality rates for some viruses can run even higher. For Nipah, a South Asian virus that triggers brain fever in humans, three out of every four infections lead to death. If the next pandemic kills people at such a rate, the results could be catastrophic.

> "What keeps me up at night is that another coronavirus like MERS [Middle East respiratory syndrome], which has a much, much higher mortality rate, becomes as transmissible as covid."[1]
>
> —Christian Walzer, executive director of health at the Wildlife Conservation Society

A Variety of Threats

Immunologists like Aronoff know that conditions in the modern world only make outbreaks of infectious disease more likely. The variety of possible threats continues to grow. Chief among these is the spillover of so-called zoonotic viruses, or animal viruses, into humans. As population rises and settlements encroach on animal habitats, the chance that an animal virus will spread to humans is greatly increased. Moreover, factors like deforestation and climate change are altering migration patterns for many species of birds, insects, and animals. Mosquito-borne illnesses such as the Zika virus and dengue fever are already spreading into new areas. Some scientists believe that the next major pandemic could be a version of avian flu, or a bird virus that infects humans.

Spillover events can also occur via the trade in animals. Researchers believe that the novel coronavirus may have crossed over from bats sold in a wet market in Wuhan, China. In such markets, exotic animals of every description, both alive and dead, are traded and sold. Factory farms present another threat from animal viruses. When large numbers of animals are stuffed into pens before slaughter, the opportunities for viral spread grow.

Infectious disease experts warn that another pandemic is almost inevitable. They cite global travel—which has become commonplace—as one way disease outbreaks race around the world within weeks.

Should a swine flu or bird flu virus become infectious to humans, a worldwide pandemic would be hard to prevent.

Experts also worry about the return of infectious diseases once thought to be almost eliminated. Crowded conditions in large cities, combined with deficient health care, can lead to fresh outbreaks of typhoid, cholera, tuberculosis, and other lethal illnesses. Failure to get vaccinations can add to the danger. In addition, there are signs that overuse of antibiotics is making these lifesaving drugs less effective.

Preparing for the Worst

Experts on infectious diseases worry about the way governments were blindsided by COVID-19. "We weren't prepared for it," admits Aronoff. "It put us on our heels."[2] To confront the next pandemic, nations must prepare for the worst. That means stocking supplies of personal protective equipment, or PPE—including gloves, masks, helmets, face shields, and goggles—to protect health care workers from infection. Experts urge adoption of protocols for contact tracing, or tracing those who have come into contact with an infected person. Smartphone apps, digital footprints, and artificial intelligence (AI) can be deployed to trace the spread of a virus with great accuracy.

Scientists are also working on widespread early warning systems to detect the first signs of a viral outbreak. Some immunologists hope to set up a worldwide database of blood samples that could conduct ongoing checks for viruses. Groups like the World Health Organization (WHO) are pushing for cooperation among member nations to avoid delays in reporting outbreaks of infectious disease. Experience shows that such delays can lead to enormous costs in human lives.

Pharmaceutical companies hope to expand on their success in developing vaccines for the coronavirus. The use of messenger RNA (mRNA) technology could lead to an array of new vaccines. mRNA is a molecule that teaches cells how to make proteins with DNA codes. In other words, it teaches cells how to reject a virus like COVID-19. Work is also proceeding on a so-called pan-virus vaccine, a single shot that would protect against a variety of viral illnesses. New methods of designing, manufacturing, and distributing vaccines could serve to stop viruses in their tracks.

The struggle to contain COVID-19 has laid bare the world's vulnerability to the next pandemic, whatever it might be. Some fear that pandemics and lockdowns could become the new normal. Nonetheless, experts like Aronoff see reasons to hope that future responses will be more effective. Scientists are making discoveries every day that could help protect against infectious disease. "We've learned lessons about how to deal with other pathogens," he says. "It's possible to be frozen in anxiety and fear about what's next, but this is what we're trained to do. We're trained to look for emerging threats and figure out how to deal with them."[3]

CHAPTER ONE

Early Warning Systems

People pay attention to authorities they respect. For example, the American public trusts the National Weather Service to forecast hazardous weather events. Some believe that a similar system could forecast, and issue warnings about, dangerous outbreaks of disease. According to Caitlin Rivers, an epidemiologist at the Johns Hopkins Center for Health Security, this kind of system could speed America's response to the next pandemic. At a May 6, 2020, appearance before a House committee on health spending, Rivers described the benefits of such a system. An agency made up of scientists, health professionals, and computer experts could monitor signs of infectious disease across the nation. It could recommend border closings or temporary lockdowns before a deadly outbreak could spread. "We don't have anything like that for outbreaks, but this [COVID-19] pandemic underscores why that must change," she said. "We should consider establishing a national center that would perform academic forecasting and analytics."[4]

The Need for a Coordinated System

Most experts agree that the United States needs a coordinated system to track outbreaks of infectious disease and create models predicting how they might spread. The pieces necessary for building a national warning system already exist. The problem is that they are scattered and do not work together. Georges C. Benjamin, executive director of the American Public Health Association, believes that Rivers's proposal would work. Benjamin notes that an online retailer like Amazon collects massive amounts of data about its customers every day. The data includes where they live, what they eat, what they do for recreation, and what their destinations are when they travel. This data could be used to create more accurate models of how disease outbreaks might move through the population. It could also help forecast other epidemics related to health care. As Benjamin notes, "If we had such a system, we would have had a better early warning on opioid epidemics, we would have had a better early warning on the obesity epidemic, we absolutely would have had a better early warning on this [COVID-19] infectious disease epidemic. All of our data systems are very silo based. They don't talk to one another, and they're not fast."[5]

> "All of our data systems are very silo based. They don't talk to one another, and they're not fast."[5]
>
> —Georges C. Benjamin, executive director of the American Public Health Association

Currently, models for infectious disease rely mostly on public health data gathered at the local level and compiled at the National Center for Health Statistics. The modelers work at universities and private foundations, while the data people reside in government offices. Rivers and others believe data collection, modeling, and forecasting for disease outbreaks should all take place under a single umbrella group—a health care version of the National Weather Service. Coordinating these tasks could allow health officials to track disease outbreaks in real time.

The MOBS Lab

Among the modelers anxious to join this effort is Alessandro Vespignani, a research scientist at Northeastern University in Boston, Massachusetts. Vespignani and his team use 1 million computer processors to create complex simulations of virus outbreaks. Their approach, however, is even more ambitious than that of most modelers. Their goal is to simulate the movements and behavior of every person on earth, or more than 7 billion individuals.

Vespignani's project is called the Laboratory for the Modeling of Biological and Socio-technical Systems, or the MOBS Lab. It seeks to overcome one of the main problems in predicting the spread of a viral disease. Data about local outbreaks, including cases and deaths, is already out of date by the time it is reported. This makes it almost useless to public health officials trying to implement measures to stop the spread. The MOBS Lab stays ahead of this information curve by predicting trends in how a virus will spread. The predictions are based on minute-by-minute information from social media, medical databases, and apps that track people's travel patterns on the ground and in the air.

The MOBS Lab looks for signals in social media that show how a virus is moving. For example, with COVID-19, its researchers found that increases in coronavirus hospitalizations and deaths in an area could be forecast from increases in Google searches for virus keywords such as "fever" or "cough." The lag time between

A health care version of the National Weather Service could speed America's response to the next pandemic. Instead of forecasting hazardous weather events, this system would forecast and issue warnings about disease outbreaks.

online searches and COVID-19 deaths averaged about twenty-one days. This is remarkably close to the twenty-day gap doctors have seen between onset of serious COVID-19 symptoms and deaths. Vespignani's team makes similar forecasts using tweets about lockdowns, quarantines, and face mask rules. They tend to show where people are planning to travel—and where the virus might bubble up next. MOBS Lab researchers even account for data that might be artificially inflated by fake news or sensational media stories that create a short-term panic. The lab continues to add data from new sources to pinpoint outbreaks with more accuracy. Among the sources are UpToDate, a fact-checking database used by medical professionals, and Kinsa Insights, a database that collects users' body temperatures.

In December 2020 Vespignani and the MOBS Lab began sharing their results with the WHO, the White House, the Centers for Disease Control and Prevention (CDC), and the Bill & Melinda Gates Foundation. The next step for the MOBS Lab is to make its data and forecasts available for public use online. This would help integrate its work with that of local health officials. Using nearly real-time data, officials could make better decisions about tightening or loosening restrictions on the basis of a viral threat. The MOBS system could help forecast trends in infectious disease weeks in advance of current methods. Mauricio Santillana, a professor at Harvard Medical School who partners with the MOBS Lab, believes that bringing health officials on board is crucial. "We've created a way to show public health officials what's going through our minds," Santillana says. "We want them to see what we see."[6]

Using the Internet of Everything

Some experts hope to go beyond simply tracking disease outbreaks. They want to derail epidemics before they get started. The solution, they believe, lies with big data, especially data produced by the so-called Internet of Everything, or IoE. With devices around the world connected to each other and talking all the time, vast amounts of data are produced, categorized, and stored. In fact, IoE records too much data for ordinary processors to handle. The data comes from smartphones and social media, geospatial tracking devices, satellite imagery, sensors on all sorts of machinery, and many other sources. Sifting this data for clues to potential outbreaks has produced a whole new field of medicine, called computation epidemiology. It employs computers powered by artificial intelligence to sort through mountains of data, looking for patterns that might reveal a possible outbreak of disease on the horizon. In this way, an unusual cluster of coughs or fevers could lead health officials to investigate.

Clues to potential outbreaks can be found in traditional places, such as doctors' diagnoses, lab samples, patient reports, and video checkups. But these sources can take weeks to compile and compare. What is more rapidly available is data pulled from linked devices like smartphones and smart watches. The Fitbit and Whoop trackers worn by runners and other people who exercise can provide hints of impending illness. Health-conscious owners use the devices to monitor heart rate, body temperature, weight loss, and other physical signs. The Apple Watch tracks its owner's sleep patterns and oxygen levels, while also giving users the option to sync their devices with other users. Amazon's digital assistant Alexa can record sneezes and coughs. Patterns of illness can be cross-checked with these results to pinpoint likely outbreaks as soon as they appear.

As the MOBS Lab noted, smartphones also track their owners' movements. They reveal where people have been and where they are going. Social media posts and airline reservations add to the mix. Technology and telecom companies can help data experts map how a pathogen travels and predict future pathways. Armed with this information, health officials can locate areas of high risk and issue real-time warnings to the public.

Scanning for Signs of Illness

Along with self-monitoring smart devices, scientists are turning to data from public monitoring systems. These systems use machine

Privacy Issues in Monitoring for Disease

The next pandemic is sure to bring concerns about privacy as governments increase surveillance to detect outbreaks. During the COVID-19 pandemic, the Chinese Communist Party (CCP) made widespread use of facial-recognition software and public security cameras to collect data on possible infections. The CCP also mandated a smartphone tracking app that used a color-coded system to govern travel. Green meant the user could move relatively freely, while red forced the person into fourteen days of quarantine. The app's 700 million users had to show their color status before boarding a train or entering a supermarket. The app also shared location data with police.

The idea of using such measures to fight a pandemic in the United States alarms those who advocate for privacy rights. Security cameras are already a feature of American daily life. New technologies can fit these devices with sensors to capture more personal information than just images. "Making this information available has [public health] uses, but it also has downsides if it is used in the wrong manner," says computer science professor Madhav Marathe. "We have to decide as a society at what point of time we are willing to give up basic rights."

Quoted in Casey Ross, "After 9/11, We Gave Up Privacy for Security. Will We Make the Same Trade-Off After Covid-19?," *StatNews*, April 8, 2020. www.statnews.com.

vision and artificial intelligence to gather and analyze health data in public settings. Machine vision refers to computerized cameras that scan the environment and inspect images for different purposes. They are placed at high-traffic areas such as airport terminals, sports arenas, and shopping malls. The visual data they collect can provide remarkable clues to possible viral infections.

Binah, an Israeli tech company, has developed software for health-related facial scanning. It employs a technology found on Fitbit devices or smart watches called remote photoplethysmography. It measures vital signs via a series of light flashes on the back of the smart device. The light flashes scan a person's skin for changes in five key vital signs. These include heart rate, respiration rate, oxygen saturation, mental stress level, and heart rate variability. Binah plans to add blood pressure monitoring as well. The software works by measuring slight variations in skin tone

that can scarcely be detected by the naked eye. It focuses on the skin above a person's cheeks, but it can gather the same data from scanning a finger.

To provide scans in public, Binah plans to set up kiosks at the entrances to malls and airports. The scanning process is not instantaneous, but it takes less than a minute. The software also works on a smartphone app for home use. During the COVID-19 pandemic, customers used the Binah app to check for signs of infection before dining or traveling. The company says its scanning software has an accuracy rate of 80 to 99 percent. Binah hopes that one day its software will be standard equipment for employees in offices and stores. The data could then be fed into a central clearinghouse to check for unusual patterns. This would allow for continuous monitoring of infectious disease.

Tracking Symptoms with AI

Experts in viral illness note that one of the first signs of coronavirus in Wuhan, China, was an uptick in patients with symptoms of respiratory illness. Coughs are a key warning sign for viral disease. Joe Brew, an epidemiologist who formerly worked for the Florida Department of Health, created a smartphone app called Hyfe to monitor coughs. Hyfe checks the sound and frequency of coughs using artificial intelligence. When the app detects an abrupt coughing noise, it records the sound and converts it to a 3-D image. This image, called a spectrogram, captures the sound's pitch and intensity. The app's AI then compares the spectrogram to a massive data set of 270,000 sounds, ranging from barks to laughs. It learns the user's unique coughing sound in order to log its variations.

Brew believes that apps like Hyfe could uncover emerging viruses with AI technology. Researchers say that patients tend to underreport how often they cough. Keeping close tabs with a smartphone app could give doctors and health officials more reliable data about symptoms. If the symptoms are linked to a deadly virus, the advance warning is crucial. It could arise long before clinics are flooded with patients and the virus is already spreading, as in the Wuhan outbreak. Moreover, the app works automatically, even when illness is the furthest thing from a person's mind. Brew notes that the worldwide expansion of smart devices makes Hyfe more useful than ever. "Cough counting would have been interesting in 1990," he says, "but right now we have some five billion humans carrying a microphone with them at all times every day, everywhere."[7]

Some also view Hyfe as a promising tool in combating old diseases that refuse to go away. Peter Small, a University of Washington expert in infectious disease, believes Hyfe could help eradicate tuberculosis (TB), a lung infection that increasingly strikes lower-income people in urban areas. Small says too many people ignore chronic coughs that can indicate TB. Hyfe's AI-run cough

> "Cough counting would have been interesting in 1990, but right now we have some five billion humans carrying a microphone with them at all times every day, everywhere."[7]
>
> —Joe Brew, an epidemiologist and creator of a cough-monitoring app

Thermal Scanners and False Alarms

Technology experts tout the use of thermal scanners in high-traffic areas to check for viral disease. During the COVID-19 pandemic, governments, schools, and private businesses invested huge sums on scanners. The manufacturers promised swift and accurate results. But IPVM, a surveillance research group, says the thermal scanners do not live up to the hype. In fact, they may be registering so many false alarms that they present a serious risk to public health.

Thermal scanning cameras work by measuring a person's skin temperature with infrared sensors. However, this measurement often does not correlate to a person's core body temperature. That is why such scanners are not approved for medical use. Moreover, their accuracy is reduced as their distance from people increases. As a result of false positives, people whose skin temperature is elevated for any number of reasons could be denied access to airplanes, supermarkets, and classrooms. There is also the problem of false negatives. Those infected with COVID-19 often showed no symptoms of viral illness despite being highly contagious themselves. "That's generally the problem with infrared imaging: It's so deceptively easy," says thermography expert Peter Plassmann. "You get a nice colorful image and you get a temperature reading. Great. But in reality, it's all rubbish."

Quoted in Drew Harwell, "Those Fever Scanners That Everyone Is Using to Fight Covid Can Be Wildly Inaccurate, Researchers Find," *Washington Post*, March 4, 2021. www.washingtonpost.com.

tracking could recommend warnings if a user's cough persists for two weeks. An automatic text could direct the person to a public clinic for testing. Just the show of concern could prevent more widespread illness. "I've been around a lot of TB patients and it's a very disconcerting diagnosis," says Small. "Even though it's almost always curable, it's psychologically difficult on patients, and having objective evidence that their cough is getting better can help with their spirits."[8]

Checking for Pathogens in Blood and Water

Another approach to tracking viruses of the future is to monitor the world's blood supply. Michael Mina, an epidemiologist at Brigham and Women's Hospital and the Harvard T.H. Chan School of Public Health, wants to test millions of blood samples for antibodies, the proteins that the human immune system makes to fight infections like viruses. His pilot project, begun in 2020, tracks anti-bodies for COVID-19 in blood samples. He hopes that a similar system could become a standard tool for detecting and fighting viral outbreaks in the future.

Mina calls his project the Global Immunological Observatory (GIO). Just as a regular observatory scans the heavens for signs of life and new planets, Mina's GIO looks for unusual concentrations of antibodies in vast numbers of blood samples. Rather than a telescope, GIO employs a microchip-powered scanning technology that can detect and analyze hundreds of thousands of antibodies in a single microliter of blood. Antibodies can reveal not only current infections but also people who have recovered from a bacterial or viral infection. The immune system produces antibodies for defense after a person has been infected for a week or two. GIO also can detect the special signature of antibodies to identify different strains of viral disease. When researchers see a jump in antibodies, whatever their target, they can flag the pathogen under attack. In this way new viruses, like the one that causes COVID-19, can be detected and cross-checked with known pathogens much faster than before. The technology can also track the movement of a virus through a population. This helps health officials plan for surges in hospital use.

"I think of the body as a constantly recording pathogen-detection device. All we have to do is tap into the hard drives, which are the plasma cells and antibodies."[9]

—Michael Mina, an epidemiologist at Brigham and Women's Hospital and the Harvard T.H. Chan School of Public Health

Mina hopes that his GIO project can be incorporated into a larger national effort to thwart potential pandemics. However, making regular blood scans to check large populations for antibodies is not cheap. Already, Mina and his team are using charitable funding to gather anonymous blood samples by the thousands. As with many early warning projects, financing for GIO remains a challenge. But Mina believes the technology is essential. "I think of the body as a constantly recording pathogen-detection device," he says. "All we have to do is tap into the hard drives, which are the plasma cells and antibodies, to better understand what's happening in our environment."[9]

Good sources for tracking future viruses include not only blood but also water. Start-up tech firm Biobot Analytics uses genetic and chemical tests plus data analytics to detect viruses and bacteria in wastewater. The Boston-based company got its start testing city sewage plants for signs of increased opioid drug use. The COVID-19 pandemic led Biobot engineers to develop a way to detect the virus in sewage. Its breakthrough brought a flood of new clients in more than four hundred cities, businesses, and universities. Biobot sends each customer a sampling kit

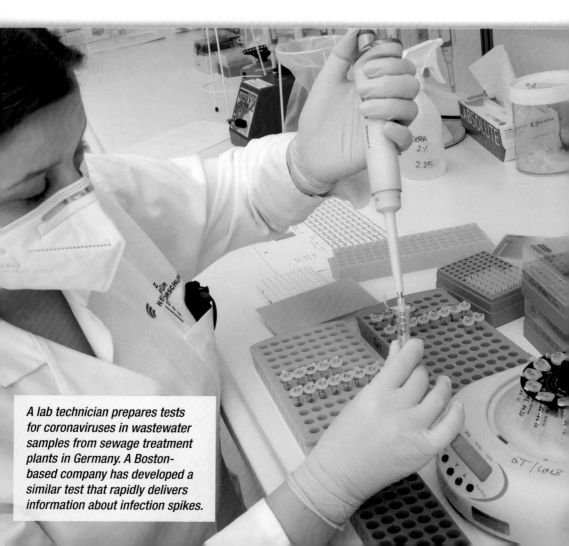

A lab technician prepares tests for coronaviruses in wastewater samples from sewage treatment plants in Germany. A Boston-based company has developed a similar test that rapidly delivers information about infection spikes.

for wastewater. The automated filtering devices are placed just above a sewer's water level. They pump sewage through special membranes that collect tiny particles of virus. The kits are then shipped back to the company's lab, where results are made available within twenty-four hours.

Biobot's wastewater testing has helped cities, towns, and universities forecast surges of infection with great accuracy. Mariana Matus, a computational biologist and Biobot cofounder, says the tests deliver information about spikes in infections more rapidly than clinics. "Wastewater largely captures people who just got infected," she says. "That's when they're shedding the most virus in poop but may not show symptoms. The beauty of this application is that you see the spike a week before you see it in the clinic."[10] Often, the tests reveal infections that the patients themselves are not yet aware of. As Biobot expands its reach, its wastewater testing promises to be an important part of any national early warning system for infectious disease.

Preventing the Next Pandemic

Experts in infectious disease hope to create a coordinated national warning system to track diseases and predict how they will spread. Such a system is needed at the national and global level. Projects like the MOBS Lab employ a huge computer capacity to create complex forecasts for the spread of viral disease. Many scientists are working on ways to use the interconnected IoE to sift clues to emerging outbreaks. Some companies are using smart devices to track symptoms of illness and warn about clusters of infection. GIO seeks to monitor the world's blood supply for antibodies that indicate viral spread. The key is to use today's gains in knowledge to prevent future pandemics. As Microsoft cofounder Bill Gates has observed, "In any crisis, leaders have two equally important responsibilities: solve the immediate problem and keep it from happening again. . . . The first point is more pressing, but the second has crucial long-term consequences."[11]

CHAPTER TWO

Testing and Treatment for the Next Pandemic

Health experts believe that improved testing could play a large role in limiting a future pandemic. An American public health researcher working in Cambodia hopes to join this worldwide effort. In January 2020 Dr. Jessica Manning noted the feverish condition of a Chinese traveler recently arrived from Wuhan. Manning suspected that the man was infected with the coronavirus and gave him a molecular test called polymerase chain reaction, or PCR. She took the patient's nasal and oral samples and ran them through a genetic sequencer. The device was an expensive new addition to Manning's makeshift lab in Phnom Penh. It reads the letters that form an organism's genetic blueprint. "I couldn't wait for the sequences to come off the sequencer," she recalls. "It was sheer giddy excitement."[12]

The man's test came back positive, making him the first coronavirus patient in Cambodia. The PCR test provided an urgent warning for a small nation with a strained health care system. It also offered clues about the still mysterious virus. The device uploaded the gene sequence to online software that compared it to many other organisms. It was almost identical to the sequence of the Wuhan virus. Manning, who works for the National Institute of Allergy and Infectious Diseases, realized that the PCR test could reveal much about the virus and how it mutated. She also saw how a sophisticated testing device in an obscure Cambodian lab could offer crucial support in the fight against the next pandemic.

A Need for Ramped-Up Testing

When COVID-19 first reached the United States, testing was the weak link in the government response. It took the CDC forty-six days to roll out a reliable PCR test, like the one Manning used in Cambodia. The CDC spent weeks on a test design that was much more complicated than the one recommended by the WHO. Thousands of the test kits were inadvertently contaminated as they were put together in CDC labs. Although quality-control checks showed a failure rate of up to 33 percent, the tainted tests were shipped to dozens of state and local public health labs. When checked by local officials, the tests did not work correctly, giving inconclusive results. At a time when ramped-up testing might have slowed the spread of the coronavirus, the federal government was scrambling to catch up. Some CDC scientists admitted they should have used the WHO model from the start. Further muddling the testing effort, a US Food and Drug Administration (FDA) rule at first prevented state and commercial labs from creating their own diagnostic tests for coronavirus. For crucial weeks at the pandemic's beginning, testing in America came to a virtual standstill. On March 1, as other nations were running millions of tests, the number of patients tested by the CDC was 1,235.

By contrast, health officials in Thailand employed a version of the WHO model and were able to diagnose eleven coronavirus infections by the end of January. When the FDA eased its rule on February 29, labs like the one at the University of Washington were able to develop their own accurate tests, processing thousands of samples a day. Health experts say the early delays by the CDC cost lives. "If we would have put [tests] out there quicker, could we have saved lives? Well sure," says Peter

C. Iwen, director of the Nebraska Public Health Laboratory in Omaha, Nebraska. "If we would have diagnosed quicker, we would have saved people."[13]

Experts say that the CDC's stumbles on diagnostic testing could be even more disastrous if faced with a deadlier virus in the future. In planning for the next pandemic, more funding is needed for rapid deployment of tests on a nationwide scale. That level of diagnostic testing calls for excess testing capacity, or more than enough from the start. Stockpiling the chemicals and equipment necessary to make testing kits available requires planning and a commitment to quality control.

Federal health officials must also take advantage of testing expertise around the country. Whether performing PCR tests or antibody tests, state and local labs can ramp up their efforts quickly. "The great strength the US has always had, not just in virology, is that we've always had a wide variety of people and groups working on any given problem," says Keith Jerome, the head of virology at the University of Washington. "When we decided all coronavirus testing had to be done by a single entity, even one as outstanding as CDC, we basically gave away our greatest strength."[14]

Increased Role for Antibody Tests

The next pandemic will likely see an increased role for serology testing, or antibody tests. These differ significantly from the PCR diagnostic tests administered by the tens of thousands during the COVID-19 outbreak. The RNA-based PCR tests examine throat and nose swabs for snippets of DNA in an active virus—in other words, a real-time illness. But antibody tests of blood samples not only identify a current infection, they also detect whether the patient has been infected in the past. Even if the virus is no longer active, the test reveals the presence of antibodies, which the immune system develops as ongoing protection. These antibodies can linger in the body long after the infection is overcome. Thus, antibody tests can provide a fuller picture of how a virus has spread through an area. By testing sample segments of a population, health officials can better estimate how many people have immunity. They can then use the information to ease lockdowns or allow businesses to reopen.

Worldwide, labs and drug companies have competed to create antibody tests. Some have been approved for commercial use. Researchers at the National Institutes of Health (NIH) and in China are seeking ways to share the results of antibody tests rapidly in order to track the progress of a pandemic. To get large-scale data, however, requires a vast expansion of serology testing, far in excess of what is currently possible.

To sidestep these limitations, a virologist at the Icahn School of Medicine at Mount Sinai in New York City has devised an alternative antibody test for labs. Florian Krammer and his team

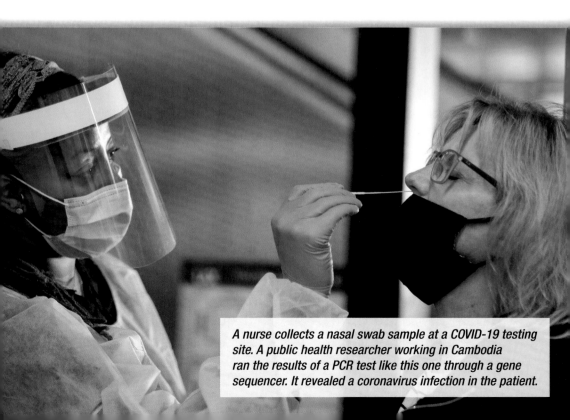

A nurse collects a nasal swab sample at a COVID-19 testing site. A public health researcher working in Cambodia ran the results of a PCR test like this one through a gene sequencer. It revealed a coronavirus infection in the patient.

developed and posted online a testing protocol that can be scaled up to screen one thousand samples a day. Krammer's antibody test uses a technique called the enzyme-linked immunosorbent assay (ELISA). It creates a chain of proteins based on a target antigen, or virus. When a patient blood or plasma sample is added to the chain, it triggers a color-coded deposit that reveals whether antibodies are present. Krammer believes the test, with its simple steps, could revolutionize antibody testing and reporting in the United States and around the world. "Our test can pick up the body's response to infection, in some cases as early as three days post-symptom onset, and is highly specific and sensitive," says Krammer. "We have shared the toolkit needed to set up the test with more than 200 research laboratories worldwide to help mitigate this global crisis."[15] On April 15, 2020, Krammer's antibody test won approval for emergency use by the FDA.

"Our [antibody] test can pick up the body's response to infection, in some cases as early as three days post-symptom onset, and is highly specific and sensitive."[15]

—Florian Krammer, a virologist at the Icahn School of Medicine at Mount Sinai in New York City

A Move to Home Testing

Faced with the sudden outbreak of a deadly pathogen, people want instant access to testing. Early in the COVID-19 outbreak, as Americans struggled to find a test for the coronavirus, they sought alternative options. Instead of the molecular PCR test, which requires clinical expertise and several hours to run, people wanted quick results. In an emergency, with labs flooded and cases exploding, waiting even a few hours can be frustrating. The situation provided an opening for companies that specialize in rapid home testing.

Support from the federal government got the ball rolling. The NIH launched a program called Rapid Acceleration of Diagnostics to develop tests that were fast, accurate, and easy to use. One of the first companies to take advantage of the program was Lucira

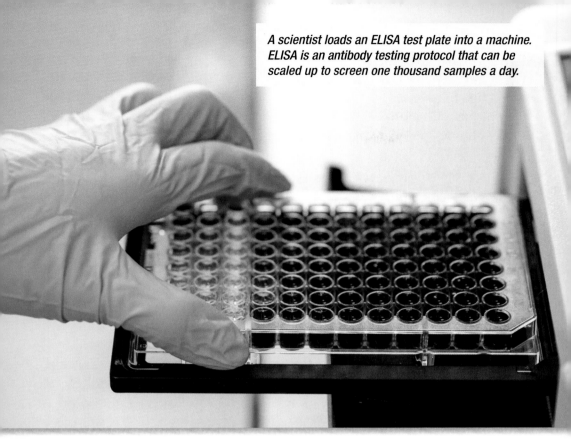

A scientist loads an ELISA test plate into a machine. ELISA is an antibody testing protocol that can be scaled up to screen one thousand samples a day.

Health, located in Emeryville, California. Lucira had already been working on a home test that could detect a person's viral infection from genetic material on a nose or throat swab. Its original target was seasonal flu, but the company jumped at the opportunity to test for COVID-19. The Lucira test, called an antigen test, does not search for the virus's molecular code. Instead, it looks for a telltale protein on the surface of the virus. Although somewhat less accurate than PCR testing, it is faster and cheaper. It is also easy for a person to administer at home.

In November 2020 the FDA approved Lucira's COVID-19 test for emergency at-home use. Rapid molecular tests from Lucira and a few other companies are currently available only in limited quantities. For now, Lucira's test is expensive at fifty dollars. But health experts assume these rapid home tests will undergo further development and be essential in battling a future pandemic. Bringing testing out of the lab and into the household could lead to earlier detection and quicker treatment—and save lives. Paul Yager, a professor in bioengineering at the University of Washington, chalks up such advances to the urgency of the COVID-19 response. "Overall, it was a very big opportunity," says Yager. "It sounds cynical, but a bad public health problem that gets everyone's attention—and certainly this got everyone's attention—pumps money into the field."[16]

Emergence of a New Antibody Therapy

The rush to treat victims of COVID-19 also highlighted new therapies that show promise for future pandemics. In early October 2020, when President Donald Trump was infected with the novel coronavirus, his physicians turned to an experimental therapy in an effort to speed his recovery. The treatment was a drug cocktail of two so-called monoclonal antibodies. The drugs, created by Regeneron Pharmaceuticals, are designed to prevent people with mild to moderate symptoms of COVID-19 from developing a severe illness. At the time, Trump was experiencing symptoms of fever and fatigue. Normally, a patient would have to wait for his or her immune system to develop antibodies against the invading virus. However, the Regeneron treatment jumps ahead by employing antibodies made in a lab to imitate the body's defenses. The drugs' effect on the immune system as the lab-made antibodies attack the coronavirus is immediate but only temporary.

Trump was hospitalized briefly, but with the help of the new drugs, he was able to recover within a week. At the time, the monoclonal antibody drugs were in clinical trials and had not yet received official approval. Regeneron provided the drugs to the president's medical team for so-called compassionate use in an emergency. Trump received 8 grams of antibodies, the highest dosage given to any trial subject. Such a treatment for an ordinary

Nanobody Therapy from the Camel Family

The next breakthrough in viral therapies might come from camels, llamas, and alpacas. These mammals share a unique characteristic. Their immune systems produce not only conventional antibodies to fight infections but also a secondary type of single-chain antibodies called nanobodies. These tiny fragments are able to bind to an antigen. Unlike larger human antibodies, however, the nanobodies can squeeze into tight spaces on viruses and in cells. Plus, they form themselves into a long chain, shaped like a finger, that helps them reach their target antigens.

Camelid nanobodies were discovered in 1989 by two Belgian graduate students. While running tests on frozen camel blood serum, the students noticed the unique characteristics of its antibodies. Since then, scientists have discovered that the nanobodies are easy to manufacture and could revolutionize antibody therapy. Twist Bioscience has created nanobody libraries, enabling researchers to test billions of nanobody sequences very quickly and at low cost. Scientists have even developed a low-dose aerosol version of nanobody therapy. Instead of getting a shot or an infusion, infected patients could inhale the spray. According to University of California, San Francisco, biochemist Peter Walter, "We anticipate it being used as a prophylactic [protective] spray before you get on an airplane or go to a party."

Quoted in Heidi Ledford, "The Race to Make COVID Antibody Therapies Cheaper and More Potent," *Nature*, October 23, 2020. www.nature.com.

patient would be enormously expensive. Nonetheless, news reports about the treatment certainly boosted the drug's profile, as did Trump's endorsement of its role in his recovery. "The fact that he was given one of these therapies has increased the awareness of them," says Dr. Mark Mulligan, director of the NYU Langone Vaccine Center. "I think in a way it's a good thing. We need some successes."[17]

On November 21, 2020, the FDA approved the Regeneron antibody drugs for general use. FDA commissioner Stephen Hahn said the monoclonal antibody therapies could help patients avoid hospitalization and ease the burden on the health care system. A similar drug made by Eli Lilly had been cleared two weeks earlier. Many experts consider monoclonal antibodies to be a promising tool in the antiviral arsenal of the future. Phase 3 clinical trials, completed in March 2021, confirmed that Regeneron's therapy works. The trials showed that it reduced hospitalization for the novel coronavirus by 70 percent.

However, the drugs remain expensive and time consuming to produce and administer. Most current antibody therapies, like Regeneron's, must be taken intravenously, like a blood transfusion. They also take time to administer: one hour for preparation, another hour for delivery by infusion, and a third hour to check for possible allergic reaction.

A More Convenient Version of Antibody Therapy

Other drug companies are determined to make a more convenient version of monoclonal antibody drugs. AstraZeneca, which has also made a vaccine for COVID-19, has developed an antibody

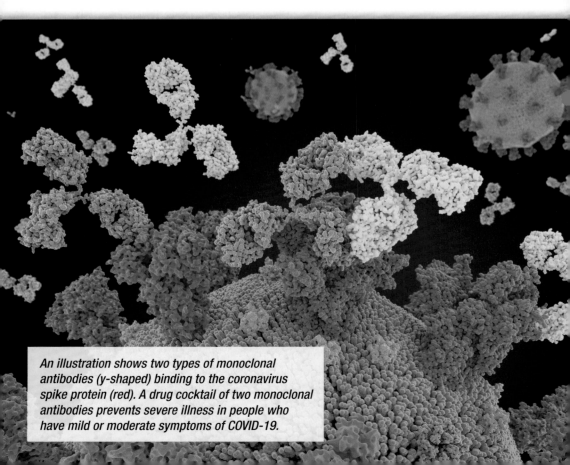

An illustration shows two types of monoclonal antibodies (y-shaped) binding to the coronavirus spike protein (red). A drug cocktail of two monoclonal antibodies prevents severe illness in people who have mild or moderate symptoms of COVID-19.

Infection Prevention for the Next Pandemic

The COVID-19 crisis has spotlighted a part of health care that is often downplayed until a new pathogen strikes. Infection prevention (IP) is bound to be crucial in facing the next pandemic. Health experts say more resources need to be devoted to IP in nursing homes, long-term care facilities, hospitals, clinics, and many other places. Protocols for curbing the spread of infections should be developed in advance so they can quickly be implemented when an outbreak appears. When COVID-19 reached the United States, health officials had to scramble to provide enough protective equipment at hospitals and other medical facilities. Offices, businesses, and restaurants received conflicting guidance on IP rules. Such delays could allow a future pathogen to spread out of control.

Nursing homes require major improvements in IP. Often a single employee is assigned IP responsibilities along with his or her other tasks. In a future pandemic, IP needs to be a focused group effort at care facilities. Moreover, Priya Nori, associate professor of medicine at Albert Einstein College of Medicine and an expert in IP procedures, thinks IP workers deserve more recognition overall. "We keep the hospital running, make sure elective surgeries can still happen," she says. "We continue to think about these things when everybody else goes to sleep at night."

Quoted in Jan Dyer, "Ready for the Next Pandemic? (Spoiler Alert: It's Coming)," *Infection Control Today*, March 1, 2021. www.infectioncontroltoday.com.

drug that can be delivered like a flu shot, with a rapid jab of a needle. AstraZeneca's idea is that getting treated for a viral illness should be just as easy as getting tested. For patients, its cocktail of two antibody drugs is literally a shot in the arm. "That changes everything because you can go get that shot at [a drugstore] and go get that shot at your doctor's office," says Michel C. Nussenzweig, an immunologist and professor at Rockefeller University in New York. "Intravenous administration is a headache. It's just a cumbersome thing to do."[18]

The strategy of providing a cocktail mixture of antibody drugs also helps guard against variants of the virus that may arise. Variants are mutated versions of a virus that can resist antibodies keyed to the original virus. In lab tests, the new antibody drugs were found to be effective against the British variant of COVID-19.

As part of Operation Warp Speed, the Trump administration bought three hundred thousand doses of both the Eli Lilly and Regeneron antibody drugs, at more than $1,250 per dose. Drugs for dealing with variants promise to be a crucial issue in future pandemics.

The next step for drug therapy is to prevent viral infection in the first place. Adagio Therapeutics, a new company, is testing a monoclonal antibody drug that not only treats infected patients but also can prevent coronavirus infection. If successful, the Adagio treatment could form a first line of defense against coronavirus outbreaks of the future. Adagio chief executive officer (CEO) Tillman Gerngross sees a long-term program of virus protection based on monoclonal antibodies. He is hopeful that one injection of the Adagio drug could protect a person for months with ready-made antibodies. "Our path to normalcy envisions a product, based on the well-known safety profile of antibodies, that can be administered twice a year," says Gerngross, "while providing greater than 90% protection against SARS-CoV-2, can be used as an effective treatment, and can offer protection against future emerging coronaviruses for everyone."[19]

To confront the next pandemic, testing and treatment must be improved and made more widely available. More funding is needed to stockpile diagnostic testing equipment and chemicals so that testing can be ramped up at the first sign of a pandemic threat. Federal health officials also need to make use of testing expertise across the nation, including antibody testing and home test kits. Treatment improvements like monoclonal antibody drugs, some delivered by simple injections, can provide ready-made antibodies to those infected with a virus. Longer term protection could come from twice-yearly antibody shots as well, giving nations one more weapon in the antiviral arsenal.

CHAPTER THREE

Creating Vaccines for the Future

One bright spot in the response to the COVID-19 pandemic has been the extraordinary success of vaccines. Drug companies were able to develop remarkably effective vaccines in under a year. Yet Richard Hatchett says that is not good enough for future pandemics. Hatchett, head of the Coalition for Epidemic Preparedness Innovations (CEPI), wants to speed up the process. For the next pandemic, he wants a vaccine ready in one hundred days, or roughly sixteen weeks.

To reach this capability, Hatchett and CEPI are calling for a five-year strategy funded by $3.5 billion in donations. What is needed, he says, is a coordinated global effort. It would require researchers, drug developers, regulators, and manufacturers all working together. Failure to take such steps, he says, could be disastrous. Hatchett notes that by the time the first COVID-19 shots were administered, about 1.5 million people had already died worldwide. And the next pandemic could be worse. "The COVID-19 pandemic is not the first pandemic of the 21st Century, and unless we act now, we can be sure that it will not be the last," says Hatchett. "There is nothing, nothing at all, to prevent the next emerging virus from being far more lethal. . . . We must shave every day we can off every step of the process if we are to deliver on the promise of the science."[20]

Rapid Response Platforms for Disease X

Officials at CEPI—like those at the WHO—refer to the next pandemic illness as Disease X. It will likely be caused by a virus that is currently unknown to physicians. It could emerge from a mutating virus or bacterium or come from a pathogen that leaps from animals to humans. COVID-19 was a Disease X, coming out of nowhere to strain national health care systems to the breaking point and kill millions. CEPI hopes to raise awareness and readiness to confront the next major outbreak of infectious disease.

In 2017 CEPI launched a global partnership to work on so-called rapid response platforms. A vaccine platform is like a backbone that forms the basis for creating specialized drugs. CEPI looked for vaccine platforms that can be rapidly adapted to meet the challenges of the next Disease X. The coalition also wanted platforms for which production can be scaled up quickly to immunize large populations.

Out of a number of proposals, CEPI officials chose to fund three rapid response platforms for vaccines. CEPI provided $34 million to the German biotech firm CureVac for development of an RNA printer. It invested $3.2 million in a partnership with Australian scientists to create a molecular clamp. A third investment of $8.4 million supported research at Imperial College London on a self-activating RNA vaccine. Researchers stress the urgent need for these and other new platforms. When the CEPI deal was signed in December 2018, Imperial College immunologist Robin Shattock said, "Next to access to clean water, vaccines have provided the greatest public health impact in human history. Today they are needed more than ever—essential to outbreak response, biosecurity, and the ever-present threat of a Disease X scenario."[21]

Today the three vaccine platform candidates remain the focus of intense re-

> "Next to access to clean water, vaccines have provided the greatest public health impact in human history. Today they are needed more than ever."[21]
>
> —Robin Shattock, an immunologist at Imperial College London

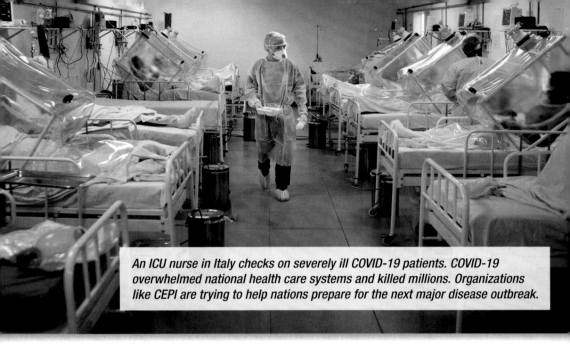

An ICU nurse in Italy checks on severely ill COVID-19 patients. COVID-19 overwhelmed national health care systems and killed millions. Organizations like CEPI are trying to help nations prepare for the next major disease outbreak.

search. These new platforms could create vaccines with great speed to protect against pathogens scientists have never seen before. As CEPI announces on its website, "We want to create a world in which epidemics are no longer a threat to humanity."[22]

Printing a Precisely Tailored Vaccine

The most promising of the CEPI-backed platforms is CureVac's RNA printer. The RNA printer does just what its name suggests. It "prints," or manufactures, a vaccine based on the instructions programmed into it. This process enables the printer to produce a vaccine that is precisely tailored to a specific pathogen. Each printer is a portable, automated unit that looks like a retro personal computer. With this platform, CureVac scientists can custom-make tiny fragments of mRNA to form the molecules required for an effective vaccine. This is the same genetic tool used in the COVID-19 vaccines from Pfizer-BioNTech and Moderna.

The RNA printer also relies on a new field called synthetic biology. This technology makes it possible to engineer molecules with great precision—and tremendous speed—simply by keying in the recipe. Since the mobile printer units can be set up anywhere, a

In September 2020 Elon Musk (left) met with German government officials to discuss the CureVac RNA printer (pictured) that his company is helping to develop.

new vaccine could be copied and printed to exact specifications in labs all over the world. This would help get vaccines into people's arms much more quickly. Among the technology's boosters is Elon Musk, CEO of electric car maker Tesla. In November 2020 Musk announced his company's agreement to continue work on an RNA vaccine bioprinter for CureVac. This is the third version on which Tesla has assisted.

Other biopharmaceutical companies are also showing success with vaccine bioprinters. Codex DNA, based in San Diego, California, used its own DNA printer to help Pfizer make its COVID-19 vaccine. With its ability to synthesize tiny DNA fragments, the Codex device was used to double-check the genetic code for Pfizer's vaccine at each step. Codex's DNA bioprinter is fully automated and barely larger than a standard desktop printer. Codex founder and CEO Todd Nelson, like the CureVac scientists, envisions a chain of bioprinters to confront new infectious diseases. According to Nelson, "If there was a network of 10,000 of these printers, we have the potential to stamp out future pandemics."[23]

Two More Vaccine Platforms for the Future

CEPI also is funding research into a vaccine platform called a molecular clamp. The technology seeks to stabilize viral surface proteins that attack healthy cells. When a virus strikes, it attaches proteins to the surface of host cells. This enables the virus to enter the cells and cause illness. These viral surface proteins are the main targets for the body's immune system, since antibodies try to block the virus's entry. However, the surface proteins are unstable and constantly change shape. Trying to eliminate them is like trying to hit a moving target. The antibodies cannot latch onto the virus firmly enough to prevent infection. To solve this problem, scientists at the University of Queensland in Australia have found a way to make synthetic copies of the surface proteins while also clamping them into a stable shape. The result is that the immune system has a stationary target it can recognize as the antigen, or foreign substance. Once purified, the synthetic antigen can be swiftly made into an effective vaccine. The Australian researchers estimate that a molecular clamp vaccine could be ready for testing within sixteen weeks of a virus's first appearance.

The Imperial College technology, dubbed RapidVac, employs so-called self-activating RNA. This means that it uses a cell's own machinery to create multiple copies of its RNA. These synthetic copies inside human cells make the antigen that spurs the immune response. Such an approach requires less vaccine and can be engineered rapidly to fight different types of viruses. Researchers say a RapidVac vaccine could also be produced in about sixteen weeks.

According to Imperial College's Shattock, the synthetic self-activating RNA-based vaccines offer the best opportunity to save lives in a future outbreak. "We want to develop Imperial's technology as a safety net to catch escape mutations, reach variants that other vaccines may not and meet potential needs for annual booster vaccinations," says Shattock. "We are also providing the UK with long-term capability in RNA vaccines for Covid-19 and other potential infectious threats."[24] RapidVac can be delivered

Profiting from Vaccine Production

Pfizer, BioNTech, Moderna, and Johnson & Johnson all stand to make huge profits from their successful COVID-19 vaccines. After all, billions of people around the world will receive one or two shots for protection against the coronavirus. In the United States the federal government guaranteed payment for the doses, ensuring profitability at the start. Yet most companies have been reluctant to enter the vaccine business. The drugs are difficult to manufacture and are tightly regulated for quality control by the FDA. Drug companies would rather focus on medicines that people take daily or once a week than on vaccines that are given once a year or once in a lifetime. In 2019 only four companies were making vaccines for the American market.

To overcome this reluctance, experts recommend more public-private partnerships like the ones for the COVID-19 vaccines. For the next pandemic, public health experts recommend that the federal government negotiate ongoing vaccine agreements with pharmaceutical companies. That way, production and distribution can ramp up quickly when necessary. Mohga Kamal-Yanni, an independent consultant on global health, believes drug companies must also accept lower profits. "Actually, the public is taking the risk," says Kamal-Yanni. "The public is paying for the cost of research and development and probably the cost of manufacturing as well."

Quoted in Jay Hancock, "They Pledged to Donate Rights to Their COVID Vaccine, Then Sold Them to Pharma," KHN, August 25, 2020. https://khn.org.

via a single-shot vaccine that provides a strong immune response with one dose. It can also be engineered as a cocktail vaccine aimed at several different pathogens.

Investing in Broad-Based Vaccines

Experts in infectious disease believe that the next generation of vaccines must offer broader protection than current versions. Should a deadly virus appear that mutates as rapidly as the human immunodeficiency virus (HIV), for example, the quest for an effective vaccine could take years. It could also result in catastrophic loss of human lives. There is still no vaccine for HIV more than forty years after it emerged in the United States. What is needed, say researchers, are pan-virus vaccines, or ones that act on multiple strains of a virus—whether HIV, coronavirus, or influenza. This would offer protection against viral variants or mutations, a problem that continues to plague health officials regarding COVID-19.

Dennis R. Burton and Eric J. Topol are urging governments and private companies to speed development of pan-virus vaccines. Burton and Topol, scientists at Scripps Research in La Jolla, California, want to focus vaccine research on so-called broadly neutralizing antibodies. This special class of antibodies can attack a wide variety of virus types. The success of mRNA vaccines against COVID-19, they note, was largely due to the unusual shape of the coronavirus's spike protein. Its structure made it fairly easy to engineer vaccines that attach to the spike protein and prevent it from invading cells. But future viruses and their mutations are likely to require a more versatile vaccine. Burton and Topol foresee a global plan to stockpile such vaccines, to be employed as soon as a new virus arises. The hope is that the neutralizing antibodies would give nations a head start in subduing an outbreak.

And what would such a broad-based stockpile strategy cost? Burton and Topol estimate that an effective system would call for investment of about $100 million to $200 million per viral outbreak. However, they believe the price tag is more than justified. As they explain in the science journal *Nature*, "As we've seen for influenza, one virus strain can cause more deaths than a world war and result in trillions of dollars of economic damage. Surely, global governments that together spend $2 trillion a year on defense can find a few hundred million dollars to stop the next pandemic?"[25]

"One virus strain can cause more deaths than a world war and result in trillions of dollars of economic damage. Surely, global governments that together spend $2 trillion a year on defense can find a few hundred million dollars to stop the next pandemic?"[25]

—Dennis R. Burton and Eric J. Topol, scientists at Scripps Research in La Jolla, California

Expanding on Existing Vaccine Platforms

When it comes to spending on vaccine research, some experts recommend doubling down on what already works. In the fight against COVID-19, mRNA vaccines from Pfizer-BioNTech and Moderna proved to be a spectacular success. They went from the drawing board to people's arms in less than a year and were up to 95 percent effective in preventing viral infection. Moderna scientists actually had the basic recipe for their vaccine ready on January 13, 2020, before the first official case had been identified in the United States. This was only two days after a lab in Wuhan, China, had posted online the genetic breakdown of the coronavirus. Moderna's team was able to input the genetic code into a previously prepared platform. Johnson & Johnson's single-shot viral vector vaccine was also developed quickly and offered a high rate of protection. The vaccines work in similar ways. The mRNA vaccine injects a string of RNA, which tells the body how to print the antigen, or target protein. The viral vector type injects an actual modified virus (usually a common cold virus) to express the antigen and trigger the body's immune response. Many researchers believe these proven approaches should form the basis for vaccine platforms of the future.

Both technologies—mRNA and viral vector—present the opportunity to "plug and play," or plug the genetic code of a new virus into an existing platform to rapidly create vaccines. Plug and play has already been tested; it is essentially how the Moderna vaccine was created. "The breakthrough here is that a platform can be used with minimal modifications to target a different virus," writes science reporter Kelsey Piper. "If a new pandemic starts with a different spike protein, researchers could rapidly develop vaccines using either of these approaches—just modifying what protein the viral vector expresses or what protein the RNA tells the body to print."[26] And while nature does throw curveballs, the evidence of recent viral epidemics follows a pattern. The viruses associated with severe acute respiratory syndrome (SARS), MERS, and COVID-19 have a number of similar properties, some of which may well be found in the next virus to emerge.

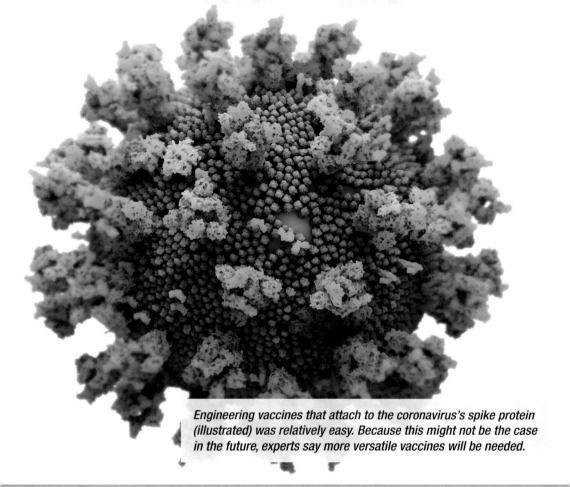

Engineering vaccines that attach to the coronavirus's spike protein (illustrated) was relatively easy. Because this might not be the case in the future, experts say more versatile vaccines will be needed.

Stretching Supply by Improving Delivery

In any future pandemic, one problem will be making a sufficient number of vaccine doses to immunize the world. That means wealthy nations must find ways to stretch the supply of vaccine. A good way to accomplish this is through new methods of vaccination. In the conventional method, a needle and syringe send the shot deep into the muscle or under the skin. However, a more efficient procedure might deliver the shot to the upper layers of the skin itself. Human skin is the body's largest organ of immune response, and it can generate a flood of immune cells, as anyone knows who has scratched a hand and seen red inflammation appear within seconds. Skin delivery can also save vaccine and thereby cover more patients. Certain new vaccination methods

Breakthrough for an Oral Vaccine

Many people have no doubt wondered, as they felt the vaccination needle sink into their arm, why a vaccine cannot be taken orally like other medicines. Scientists at Esperovax, a biotech firm in Michigan, apparently have been wondering the same thing. They have created an mRNA-based vaccine that can be swallowed as a pill or capsule. The mRNA in the oral vaccine is synthesized moments before it reaches the immune cells in a person's small intestine. Then it makes the antigen that attracts the immune response, as with other vaccines.

The Esperovax vaccine employs a type of yeast used in baking, brewing, and wine making to deliver its RNA cells to the small intestine at low cost. The company notes that with the amount of yeast that brewers produce in a day, it could immunize the world's population sixty-eight times. The oral vaccine can be manufactured rapidly and remains stable on the shelf. Esperovax CEO David O'Hagan sees the oral vaccine as a game changer. "Taking a pill or gummy is less intimidating than being poked with a needle," says O'Hagan. "We expect this approach will lead to safer, more effective vaccines, and that it will reduce the fear of the vaccination process."

Quoted in MaryAnn Labant, "The Sleeping Giants of Vaccine Production Awaken," *Genetic Engineering & Biotechnology News*, February 3, 2021. www.genengnews.com.

even dispense with normal-size needles altogether. Children, not to mention many adults, tend to appreciate the lack of a jab.

Today skin vaccination can be done with microneedle patches. The patch—often no larger than a fingertip—is placed on a person's hand or arm, and within a few minutes the vaccination is complete. Hundreds of tiny needles deliver the drug into the skin painlessly. The needles, made of sugar, then dissolve into the skin. Another version sinks a vaccine-filled tube of sugars, tinier than one grain of rice, under the skin.

Skin vaccination offers many advantages over traditional methods. Microneedle patches need not be stored at freezing temperatures and in fact are not affected by heat, meaning the patches can be kept in ordinary warehouses year-round. The patches generally use one-sixth the amount of vaccine in a typical syringe shot, yet they provide full immune response.

Microneedle patches also require less training for delivery. Some could easily be self-administered at home. This would help reduce crowding at vaccination sites, thus limiting new infections during a pandemic. Researchers have even suggested that future vaccination programs could be conducted by mail, ensuring that people receive their patches at regular intervals. "What you really want is to get the vaccine to the people and not have the people come to the vaccine,"[27] says David Hoey, CEO of Vaxxas, an Australian developer.

CEPI has recruited researchers, regulators, and manufacturers around the world as part of its five-year plan to rapidly develop vaccines for future pandemics. Experts at CEPI believe the best way to speed up the creation and delivery of vaccines is to maintain platforms for rapid response. These vaccine platforms could be adapted to address any new viral threat within one hundred days. Other researchers are also at work on broad-based vaccines that can deal with multiple strains of a basic virus. Funding is key to these platform-based efforts. The success of COVID-19 vaccines, produced through public-private partnerships, continues to inspire more innovations to confront the next pandemic.

"What you really want is to get the vaccine to the people and not have the people come to the vaccine."[27]

—David Hoey, CEO of Vaxxas, an Australian developer of vaccine delivery systems

CHAPTER FOUR

Viruses That Cross from Animals to Humans

In a remote rain forest in Africa, Yanthe Nobel is hunting for viruses. A veterinarian and a PhD student in epidemiology, she has traveled to the Dzanga-Sangha Special Reserve in the Central African Republic to search for animal viruses, the kind that could pose a threat to humans. Notified about a dead elephant in the area, she finds the corpse and dons protective gear before examining it. The elephant is a baby, and the reason for its death is uncertain. Nobel takes tissue samples and heads back to camp. Later she will shower under a waterfall and then test the samples for pathogens. Nobel's work is dangerous, filled with constant peril from armed poachers, stampeding herds, and tropical diseases. Nonetheless, she knows that her research could help prevent a future pandemic like the one unfolding in the outside world.

Nobel is seeking signs of zoonotic spillover, in which an animal virus crosses over to infect humans. SARS-CoV-2, the coronavirus that causes COVID-19, is a prime example of a zoonotic virus. Originating in or around Wuhan, China, it seems to have jumped from a bat to a person, perhaps by way of an intermediate mammal. The threat from the novel coronavirus has been all the worse because it emerged so suddenly and so little was known about it. Zoonotic viruses cause a range of illnesses, including AIDS, SARS, MERS,

Ebola, Zika, and swine flu. According to epidemiologists, about three new zoonotic viruses appear every year. And zoonotic outbreaks have increased in the past thirty years. "As a veterinarian, I am already trained to see the danger of spillovers from animals to people," says Nobel, who studies zoonotic disease at the Robert Koch Institute's Leendertz Lab. "People are waking up to a story that was already there."[28]

"As a veterinarian, I am already trained to see the danger of spillovers from animals to people. People are waking up to a story that was already there."[28]

—Yanthe Nobel, a veterinarian and PhD student in epidemiology

Spillover at the Edge

The Dzanga-Sangha Special Reserve is an ideal location for Noble's zoonotic research. It forms a boundary between the animal kingdom and human civilization. In this rain forest outpost, where poachers roam at will, the likelihood of a virus crossing over from an animal carcass to a person increases. Researchers like Nobel fan out every day across forests and jungles and deep into caves, in search of clues about zoonotic spillover. Each time Nobel comes upon a dead animal, she carefully takes samples for a biopsy. If her own tests do not reveal any recognizable pathogens, she sends the samples to a more sophisticated lab in Germany. Catalogued for research, the samples might one day hold the key to a lifesaving treatment or vaccine.

Another reason that areas like the Dzanga-Sangha preserve are ripe hunting grounds for viruses lies with the diversity of species found there. "Tropical rainforests are exceptionally important in this regard," says Dr. Tom Gillespie, who heads a lab at Emory University in Atlanta, Georgia, that studies pathogens and environmental change. "Here you have a diversity of bats, rodents, primates—the species where we are most likely to contract something—[so] you are going to have a diversity of pathogens as well."[29]

However, as people and settlements push their way into animal habitats, the boundary between animals and humans keeps

Elephants roam in the Dzanga-Sangha Special Reserve in the Central African Republic. The reserve is an ideal location for research on animal viruses that could infect humans as it forms a boundary between the animal kingdom and human civilization.

moving. Population growth, deforestation, oil and gas exploration, mining, hunting, and illegal trade in animals all contribute to the mingling of species. Habitats can also be altered due to climate change or catastrophic weather events such as floods or droughts. Habitat edges or boundaries, where the danger of zoonotic spillover is greatest, are mostly located in Africa and Asia. Yet most of the labs that screen for animal viruses are found in Europe and North America. To prevent the next zoonotic-based pandemic, more fieldwork must be conducted across still-wild habitats by scientists like Nobel.

Screening Wildlife Markets for Viruses

A group of scientists hope to build on the work of field researchers like Nobel. They call themselves the Wildlife Disease Surveillance Focus Group. The members include wildlife biologists, ecologists, and experts in infectious disease. They envision a global surveillance network to screen wild animals for possible viruses at wildlife markets where animals are sold. Among these animals are exotic species that are purchased for food or to keep as pets. The markets are a ripe source of viruses that could cross over into the human population. And people have no natural immunity against a virus that does manage to cross over. This danger drives the group's mission. Jennifer A. Philips, codirector of the Division of Infectious Diseases at Washington University School of Medicine in St. Louis, Missouri, notes that three different coronaviruses have spilled over to humans in the past twenty years. "Even a decade ago it would have been difficult to conduct worldwide surveillance at the human-wildlife interface," says Philips, who helped organize the surveillance group. "But because of technological advances, it is now feasible and affordable, and it has never been more obvious how necessary it is."[30]

Under the group's plan, regional teams of researchers and technicians would extract genome samples from market animals. Each sample could then be sequenced on-site and the gene sequences uploaded to a central database. With equipment prices falling, such screenings could be done even in areas with limited resources. Someday soon, upon the appearance of a new zoonotic virus, scientists could check for matches in a global database filled with genetic codes for animal viruses. Most important, they could identify whether an animal virus has genes linked to disease-causing pathogens in humans. The new system would be safer and easier than current methods of fieldwork. According to Gideon Erkenswick, one of the surveillance group's founding members:

> There's now a genetic sequencer available that is literally the size of a USB stick. You could bring that and a few other supplies into a rainforest and analyze a sample . . . on site in a matter of hours. I mean, if you do chance upon something like the virus that causes COVID-19, do you really want

to be collecting it, storing it, transporting it, risking further exposure, . . . and adding months or years of delay, before you figure out what you've got? There are people with the expertise and skills to do this kind of work safely pretty much everywhere in the world, they just haven't been given the tools.[31]

The Global Virome Project

Dennis Carroll, a longtime public health adviser on infectious disease, nurses an even more ambitious scheme for cataloging the world's viruses. At present, virologists have identified only about 4,000 of the more than 1.67 million viruses assumed to be lurking on earth. Carroll, however, seeks to go far beyond current efforts. Over the next ten years, he hopes to recruit a global

How Viruses Jump from Animals to Humans

Many scientists agree that the next pandemic is likely to come from another zoonotic spillover event. In general, for an animal virus to infect humans requires uniquely favorable circumstances. Like human-to-human infections, crossovers generally occur due to close contact with body fluids, including blood, mucus, feces, and urine.

Each virus in nature evolves to target one specific species. As a result, it is rare for a virus to jump to another species and be able to infect it. This happens only by chance and after long contact with the virus. At first, because the virus is not well adapted to infect its new host, it spreads slowly and with difficulty. However, as time passes, the virus may be able to mutate and produce variants that are better suited to the new host.

When an animal virus evolves to infect a human, the disease is often much more severe. This is because the human host has to tackle an invader for which it has no immunity. As epidemiologist Christine Kreuder Johnson notes, "The entire world population, for the most part, is naïve to this new virus because none of us have been exposed to it before. And that's what makes it especially dangerous."

Quoted in Justine Calma, "To Prevent the Next Pandemic, Scientists Search for Animal Zero," The Verge, April 10, 2020. www.theverge.com.

network of scientists to collect hundreds of thousands of viruses from animal samples in the wild. The viruses' genomes, or virome, could then be mapped and cataloged. Carroll estimates that the project, called the Global Virome Project, will cost $1.2 billion.

Many experts in virology question the need to cast the net so widely. They also reject the expense. Only a few zoonotic viruses, they say, present an actual danger to humans. The trick is identifying which ones pose the likeliest threat. Nevertheless, Carroll remains committed to his plan. He claims that its main attraction is being proactive. "We know that all future viral threats already exist and they are circulating in wildlife," he says. "Rather than waiting for that future threat to spill over into us and then become aware of it and react to it, the Global Virome Project is about going out into the population of wildlife and documenting and characterizing what is out there."[32]

The seventy-one-year-old Carroll does not lack for experience in the field. In 2009 he helped set up a program called PREDICT for the US Agency for International Development. The program sought to forecast which animal viruses were most likely to spill over and cause zoonotic infections in humans. Along the way, PREDICT named about twelve hundred new viruses, trained thousands of fieldworkers in more than thirty nations, and assisted in building sixty viral labs around the world. It remains one of the most successful projects to address zoonotic spillover.

Carroll launched the Global Virome Project in 2019, just before COVID-19 took center stage among epidemiologists and wildlife researchers. Since then he has been raising money from private foundations and governments. Special support has been solicited from the governments of China and Thailand. Animal sampling

"Rather than waiting for that future threat to spill over into us and then become aware of it and react to it, the Global Virome Project is about going out into the population of wildlife and documenting and characterizing what is out there."[32]

—Dennis Carroll, head of the Global Virome Project

and screening in those and similar nations, where wildlife and humans intersect regularly, is crucial to Carroll's vision. Despite criticism from skeptics, Carroll intends to continue his comprehensive approach to cataloging viruses through the Global Virome Project.

Horseshoe Bats and Wildlife Markets

Among wildlife sources for a future pandemic, bats remain likely suspects. Scientists originally blamed the novel coronavirus outbreak in Wuhan on a virus from horseshoe bats that somehow found its way to a local seafood market. The outdoor market featured all kinds of exotic animals, both alive and dead. Some experts theorized that a virus from a horseshoe bat could have passed to an intermediate mammal—in this case a pangolin, or scaly anteater—before somehow infecting people at the market. A joint study by the WHO and Chinese officials, released in March 2021, claims that this is the likeliest explanation of COVID-19's origin. Other scientists have cast doubt on this theory, since the nearest bats in question reside in caves more than 1,000 miles (1,609 km) from Wuhan.

At any rate, contaminated animals at outdoor markets remain a concern as sources of zoonotic spillover. Carroll considers markets like the one in Wuhan to be a threat for spreading viruses that cross over. "In Wuhan, clearly the bringing in of wildlife and mixing them with livestock and exposing them to people while animals are still alive poses enhanced risk," he says. "There are biosecurity measures to reduce the risk of viruses moving into livestock or into people."[33]

Many infectious disease experts focus on bats as the greatest risk. Bats are in a class by themselves as carriers of viruses capable of jumping to other species. Not even rodents host so many viruses, and more than sixty bat viruses are known to infect humans. SARS, Ebola, and Nipah all seem to have originated in bats. Bats also have what scientists call sympathy, or the tendency to share viruses with other species of bats. This ensures that bat viruses spread more widely and offers more chances for zoonotic spillover to humans.

The origins of COVID-19 are still being studied. One theory is that it came from horseshoe bats that were being sold in a wet market in Wuhan, China. One variety of horseshoe bat is pictured.

Not surprisingly, much research on how pathogens spread and mutate centers on bat viruses. The Wuhan Institute of Virology, located just 9 miles (14.5 km) from the seafood market linked to COVID-19, hosts some of the world's foremost work on bat viruses. Its director, Shi Zhengli, has been dubbed the "bat woman" for her focus on coronaviruses in bats. Part of this work is so-called gain-of-function research. This seeks to determine how an animal virus can infect humans, in part by modifying the virus and making it deadlier or more infectious. Some experts in virology, while admitting the research is dangerous, consider it important. Others question whether the benefits outweigh the risks. "I haven't seen any of the vaccine companies say that they need to do this work in order to make vaccines," says Thomas Inglesby, director of the Johns Hopkins Center for Health Security. "I have not seen evidence that the information people are pursuing could be put into widespread use in the field."[34]

There are also questions about the safety protocols the Wuhan lab maintains in its research. Nicholas Wade, a former science

In Defense of Bats

In the early weeks of the COVID-19 pandemic, villagers in Rajasthan, a state in northern India, decided to take revenge against those they held responsible for the outbreak. Crowds gathered at an abandoned fort to throw stones and beat the offenders with sticks. Their targets were bats, hundreds of them clinging to the eaves of the old structure. News reports had informed the people that the novel coronavirus likely passed into humans from horseshoe bats in China.

Scientists say it is hardly the bats' fault that they spread viruses to people. Bats are not aggressive and prefer to keep their distance, but the forests where they live keep shrinking due to human activity. Researchers say bats have unique immune systems that enable them to carry viruses that can kill humans and livestock but have little effect on the bats themselves. Scientists hope to unlock the secrets of the bats' immune system to better understand how they shed viral matter. Some theorize it has to do with stress. "Stress is a huge factor in upsetting the natural balance that bats have with their viruses," says virologist Vikram Misra. "The more you stress bats, the more they shed viruses."

Quoted in "Scientists Look at Bats to Find Early Signs of the Next Pandemic," *Deccan Herald* (Bangalore, India), December 14, 2020. www.deccanherald.com.

columnist at the *New York Times,* claims that the Wuhan lab relaxed its safety standards to a Level 2, with Level 4 being the most stringent. Wade is among a growing number of people, including some scientists, who believe that the COVID-19 virus may have escaped from the Wuhan virology lab. To avert the next pandemic, scientists around the world have sounded alarms about safety standards in the study of zoonotic viruses.

The One Health Initiative

Increasingly, scientists and physicians are stressing the interconnectedness of species in addressing zoonotic events. For example, if a dog should die of Rocky Mountain spotted fever, it is unusual for a veterinarian to inquire about the owner's health. The owner's doctor might never hear about the infection. Yet the disease could result in human cases that might even prove fatal. "When veterinarians see potentially infectious diseases, there's no way for them to communicate with local medical providers," says Peter Rabinowitz, director of the Center for One Health Research at the University of Washington. "What they do now is tell the patient to talk to their doctor, and that may not be the most efficient way of communicating an emerging threat."[35]

This demonstrates the need to see the larger picture of public health and ways to prevent infectious disease. The CDC calls the approach One Health. The idea is that different disciplines, from veterinary medicine to immunology, should work together at the local, national, and international level. Advocates believe the result would be improved health for humans, animals, and the earth's environment.

Followers of the One Health Initiative often cite Rudolf Virchow, a nineteenth-century German scientist and thinker who coined the term *zoonoses* for diseases that jump from animals to people. "Between animal and human medicine there are no dividing lines," said Virchow, "nor should there be."[36] Scientists note that while viruses like HIV can cross over from chimpanzees, humans also can transmit pathogens like the novel coronavirus to apes. In January 2021, for example, two gorillas at the San Diego Zoo Safari Park tested positive for the coronavirus.

Just as viruses can cross over from animals to humans, they can also be transmitted from humans to animals. In January 2021 two gorillas at the San Diego Zoo Safari Park tested positive for the coronavirus. (One of the Safari Park's many gorillas is pictured.)

Park officials suggested the gorillas contracted the virus from an asymptomatic park worker.

Zoonotic events have become more frequent due to factors such as human population growth and spread, climate change, and destruction of animal habitats. Although many health officials already support the One Health approach, most governments have yet to include its insights in their disease-control policies. In contemplating the next pandemic—perhaps from a bat-borne virus or perhaps from some unknown source—governments need to reckon costs in the trillions. "We have high human population densities, high livestock densities, high rates of deforestation— and these things are bringing bats and people into closer contact," says Raina Plowright, a virus researcher at the Bozeman Disease Ecology Lab in Montana. "We are rolling the dice faster and faster and more and more often. It's really quite simple."[37]

SOURCE NOTES

Introduction: An Eye on Future Pandemics

1. Quoted in Jim Robbins, "Heading Off the Next Pandemic," KHN, January 4, 2021. https://khn.org.
2. Quoted in Jan Dyer, "Ready for the Next Pandemic? (Spoiler Alert: It's Coming)," *Infection Control Today*, March 1, 2021. www.infectioncontroltoday.com.
3. Quoted in Dyer, "Ready for the Next Pandemic?"

Chapter One: Early Warning Systems

4. Quoted in Jeannie Baumann, "Pandemic 'Weather Service' Key Before Next Outbreak, House Told," Bloomberg Law, May 6, 2020. https://news.bloomberglaw.com.
5. Quoted in Baumann, "Pandemic 'Weather Service' Key Before Next Outbreak, House Told."
6. Quoted in Emily Arntsen, "These Researchers Are Predicting COVID-19 Trends Weeks Before Standard Surveillance," News @ Northeastern, March 9, 2021. http://news.northeastern.edu.
7. Quoted in Max Kozlov, "AI-Assisted Cough Tracking Could Help Detect the Next Pandemic," *The Scientist*, December 6, 2020. www.the-scientist.com.
8. Quoted in Kozlov, "AI-Assisted Cough Tracking Could Help Detect the Next Pandemic."
9. Quoted in Jerimiah Oetting, "Forecasting the Next COVID-19," Princeton University, December 14, 2020. www.princeton.edu.
10. Quoted in Adam Bluestein, "Biobot Analytics Knows If You Have COVID-19 Before You Do—from Your Poop," *Fast Company*, March 9, 2021. www.fastcompany.com.
11. Quoted in Anette Breindl, "The Next Pandemic: Death, Taxes and Zoonotic Spillover," BioWorld, April 7, 2020. www.bioworld.com.

Chapter Two: Testing and Treatment for the Next Pandemic

12. Quoted in Amos Zeeberg, "Piecing Together the Next Pandemic," *New York Times*, February 16, 2021. www.nytimes.com.
13. Quoted in David Willman, "The CDC's Failed Race Against Covid-19: A Threat Underestimated and a Test Overcomplicated," *Washington Post*, December 26, 2020. www.washingtonpost.com.
14. Quoted in Neel V. Patel, "Why the CDC Botched Its Coronavirus Testing," *MIT Technology Review*, March 5, 2020. www.technologyreview.com.
15. Quoted in Mount Sinai, "Mount Sinai's Blood Test to Detect Antibodies to COVID-19 Receives Emergency Use Authorization from U.S. Food and Drug Administration," April 15, 2020. www.mountsinai.org.
16. Quoted in Nicole Wetsman, "COVID-19 Took Disease Tests Out of the Lab—and May Keep Them There," The Verge, March 10, 2021. www.theverge.com.
17. Quoted in Katie Thomas and Denise Grady, "Trump's Testimonial Is a Double-Edged Sword for Regeneron," *New York Times*, October 13, 2020. www.nytimes.com.
18. Quoted in Joseph Walker, "Companies Race to Develop Drugs That Stay Ahead of Coronavirus Mutations," *Wall Street Journal*, January 19, 2021. www.wsj.com.
19. Quoted in Amirah Al Idrus, "Adagio Debuts with $50M to Fight COVID-19—and the Next Pandemic," FierceBiotech, July 16, 2020. www.fiecebiotech.com.

Chapter Three: Creating Vaccines for the Future

20. Quoted in Kate Kelland, "Vaccine 'Revolution' Could See Shots for Next Pandemic in 100 Days," Reuters, March 10, 2021. www.reuters.com.
21. Quoted in Mario Christodoulou, "CEPI Partners with Imperial College to Develop Transformative Rapid-Response Technology to Create Vaccines Against Emerging Infectious Diseases," CEPI, December 10, 2018. https://cepi.net.
22. CEPI, "New Vaccines for a Safer World," April 30, 2021. https://cepi.net.
23. Quoted in Mary Ellen Schneider, "Codex DNA Takes Vaccine Printing from Concept to Reality," BioWorld, September 1, 2020. www.bioworld.com.

24. Quoted in Clive Cookson, "Imperial College to Target Coronavirus Mutations," *Financial Times* (London), January 26, 2021. www.ft .com.
25. Dennis R. Burton and Eric J. Topol, "Variant-Proof Vaccines—Invest Now for the Next Pandemic," *Nature*, February 8, 2021. www.na ture.com.
26. Kelsey Piper, "How to Develop Vaccines Faster Before the Next Pandemic," Vox, April 14, 2021. www.vox.com.
27. Quoted in Jason Douglas, "A Covid-19 Vaccine Without a Needle? These Firms Are on the Case," *Wall Street Journal*, March 3, 2021. www.wsj.com.

Chapter Four: Viruses That Cross from Animals to Humans

28. Quoted in Leslie Hook, "The Next Pandemic: Where Is It Coming from and How Do We Stop It?," *Financial Times* (London), October 29, 2020. www.ft.com.
29. Quoted in Hook, "The Next Pandemic."
30. Quoted in Tamara Bhandari, "Global Wildlife Surveillance Could Provide Early Warning for Next Pandemic," The Source, July 9, 2020. https://source.wustl.edu.
31. Quoted in Bhandari, "Global Wildlife Surveillance Could Provide Early Warning for Next Pandemic."
32. Quoted in Jim Robbins, "Before the Next Pandemic, an Ambitious Push to Catalog Viruses in Wildlife," Yale Environment 360, April 22, 2020. https://e360.yale.edu.
33. Quoted in Robbins, "Before the Next Pandemic, an Ambitious Push to Catalog Viruses in Wildlife."
34. Quoted in Kelsey Piper, "Why Some Labs Work on Making Viruses Deadlier—and Why They Should Stop," Vox, May 1, 2020. www .vox.com.
35. Quoted in *Infectious Disease News*, "One Health Approach Essential to Controlling Public Health Threats," April 2017. www.healio .com.
36. Quoted in *Infectious Disease News*, "One Health Approach Essential to Controlling Public Health Threats."
37. Quoted in Jim Robbins, "Heading Off the Next Pandemic," KHN, January 4, 2021. www.khn.org.

FOR FURTHER RESEARCH

Books

Warren A. Andiman, *Animal Viruses and Humans: A Narrow Divide; How Lethal Zoonotic Viruses Spill Over and Threaten Us*. Philadelphia, PA: Paul Dry, 2018.

Laurie Garrett, *The Coming Plague: Newly Emerging Diseases in a World Out of Balance*. New York: Picador, 2020.

Peter J. Hotez, *Preventing the Next Pandemic: Vaccine Diplomacy in a Time of Anti-Science*. Baltimore, MD: Johns Hopkins University Press, 2021.

David Quammen, *Spillover: Animal Infections and the Next Human Pandemic*. New York: Norton, 2013.

Steven Taylor, *The Psychology of Pandemics: Preparing for the Next Global Outbreak of Infectious Disease*. Newcastle upon Tyne, UK: Cambridge Scholars, 2019.

Internet Sources

Linda Givetash, "Preventing the Next Pandemic Will Cost $22.2 Billion a Year, Scientists Say," NBC News, July 23, 2020. www.nbcnews.com.

Leslie Hook, "The Next Pandemic: Where Is It Coming from and How Do We Stop It?," *Financial Times* (London), October 29, 2020. www.ft.com.

Jennifer Kahn, "How Scientists Could Stop the Next Pandemic Before It Starts," *New York Times*, April 21, 2021. www.nytimes.com.

Kate Kelland, "Vaccine 'Revolution' Could See Shots for Next Pandemic in 100 Days," Reuters, March 10, 2021. www.reuters.com.

Jim Robbins, "Heading Off the Next Pandemic," KHN, January 4, 2021. https://khn.org.

Organizations and Websites

Brookings Institution
www.brookings.edu
The Brookings Institution is a think tank that brings together experts in government and academia from all over the world to pro-

vide research, policy recommendations, and analysis on a full range of public policy issues. The institution's website features many articles and analyses on how to deal with future pandemics, including "Preventing the Next Zoonotic Pandemic."

Centers for Disease Control and Prevention (CDC)
www.cdc.gov
The CDC works around the clock to protect America from health, safety, and security threats, both foreign and in the United States. The CDC website contains abundant information on vaccines and therapies that will be instrumental in fighting future pandemics.

Global Virome Project (GVP)
www.globalviromeproject.org
The GVP is a collaborative scientific initiative to discover zoonotic viral threats and stop future pandemics. The GVP's website describes its mission in detail and includes news articles and information about efforts to detect zoonotic spillover and ways to prepare for future outbreaks.

The Heritage Foundation (HF)
www.heritage.org
The Heritage Foundation performs research and pursues solutions to support freedom, opportunity, and prosperity in America. The foundation's work on pandemic disease includes "A New Strategy for Equipping Medical Providers to Cope with the Next Pandemic or Infectious-Disease Outbreak."

US Food and Drug Administration (FDA)
www.fda.gov
The FDA helps protect the public health by ensuring the safety, efficacy, and security of drugs, biological products, and medical devices, as well as the nation's food supply and cosmetics. The FDA website contains valuable information about testing and approving vaccines for the next pandemic.

INDEX

PICTURE CREDITS

ABOUT THE AUTHOR

John Allen is a writer who lives in Oklahoma City.